Favorite Fairy Tales

TOLD IN SWEDEN

Favorite Fairy Tales

TOLD
IN
SWEDEN

Retold
by
VIRGINIA HAVILAND

Illustrated
by
RONNI SOLBERT

Boston LITTLE, BROWN AND COMPANY *Toronto*

These stories have been retold from the following sources:

THE BOY AND THE WATER-SPRITE is retold from SVENSKA FOLKSAGOR
OCH ÄFVENTYR by Gunnar Olof Hyltén-Cavallius and George
Stephens, as translated in 1964 by Jennifer Waldén from the ver-
sion of Elsa Olenius in I SAGANSSKOG (Stockholm, AB Rabén &
Sjögrens Bokförlag, 1954).

THE OLD WOMAN AND THE TRAMP, THE LAD AND THE FOX, THE OLD
WOMAN AND THE FISH, and LARS, MY LAD! are retold from FAIRY
TALES FROM THE SWEDISH by Nils Gabriel Djurklou (New York,
F. A. Stokes Co., 1901), translated by H. L. Braekstad.

PINKEL is retold from SVENSKA FOLKSAGOR, edited by Fridtjuv Berg
(Stockholm, Svensk Lärenetidnings Förlag, Vol. 2, 1903), translated in 1964 by Jennifer Waldén.

Published simultaneously in Canada
by Little, Brown & Company (Canada) Limited

PRINTED IN THE UNITED STATES OF AMERICA

Contents

THE BOY AND THE WATER-SPRITE 3

THE OLD WOMAN AND THE TRAMP 15

THE LAD AND THE FOX 30

PINKEL 33

THE OLD WOMAN AND THE FISH 50

LARS, MY LAD! 60

The Boy and the Water-Sprite

ONCE UPON A TIME there were three brothers whose parents had died without leaving much to be divided among the three. Nor was their inheritance fairly shared. The eldest son took the cottage and the second son took all that was in it. Nothing remained for the youngest son but some rope that he found piled in a corner.

This rope will always be useful for something, he thought. He took it away and made snares of it.

With the snares he soon caught a squirrel, and then a hare. Next he went down to the shore of the lake, where a bear lay sleeping in his rocky lair. The boy sat down on the beach and knotted another, larger snare with which to catch the bear. While he was doing this, a water-sprite came up through the lake and watched him curiously. Then he went down again and sent up his son, a wee water-sprite, to find out what the stranger was doing with the rope.

"Oh!" said the boy, in answer to the little water-sprite. "I am going to tie up the whole lake so that nobody can come up out of the water."

The wee water-sprite hurried down to tell this to his father.

"Go back again," said the water-sprite, "and ask him if he can race as fast as you to the top of the tall tree. When you have caught up with him, just shove him down into the lake and we shall be rid of him."

The wee water-sprite went back up through the water as his father ordered and invited the boy to race with him up the tree.

"I can't be bothered to," answered the boy, "but I have a little fellow with me and if he wants to race with you, he shall."

The boy freed the squirrel from his snare. When the little water-sprite tried to overtake it, he was left far behind. He ran back to his father and told him what had happened.

"Go back again," said the water-sprite, "and ask the boy if he will run a race with you. When he is tired, drag him into the lake and we shall be rid of him."

The wee water-sprite again went up through the water, as his father ordered, and invited the boy to race with him.

"I can't be bothered to," answered the boy, "but I have a little fellow with me, a bit bigger than the other one, and if he wants to race with you, I don't mind. When he's tired, I'll take over."

He freed the hare now, and it shot away so fast that the little water-sprite hardly caught a glimpse of its long ears.

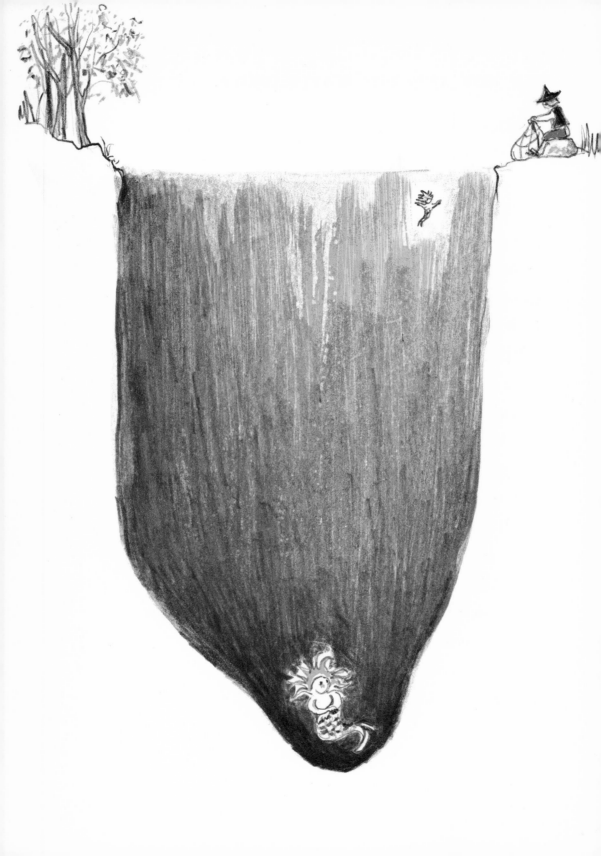

When the water-sprite heard about this he said, "Go back again and ask the boy if he would like to wrestle with you. When you have him on the ground, just drag him down into the lake and then we shall be rid of him."

Once more the wee water-sprite returned, as his father ordered, and invited the boy to wrestle with him.

"I can't be bothered to," answered the boy, "but if you really feel like fighting, you might challenge old Grandpa. He is lying in that cave. At first he may be a bit sleepy, but cuff him on the ear and that will wake him up."

The little water-sprite went to the lair and asked old Grandpa if he would like to come out and have a tussle. But the bear was too lazy to move and only growled a bit.

"Now then, no growling!" said the little water-sprite, and gave him a real whack.

The bear stood up then and with his great paw hit the little water-sprite such a blow that

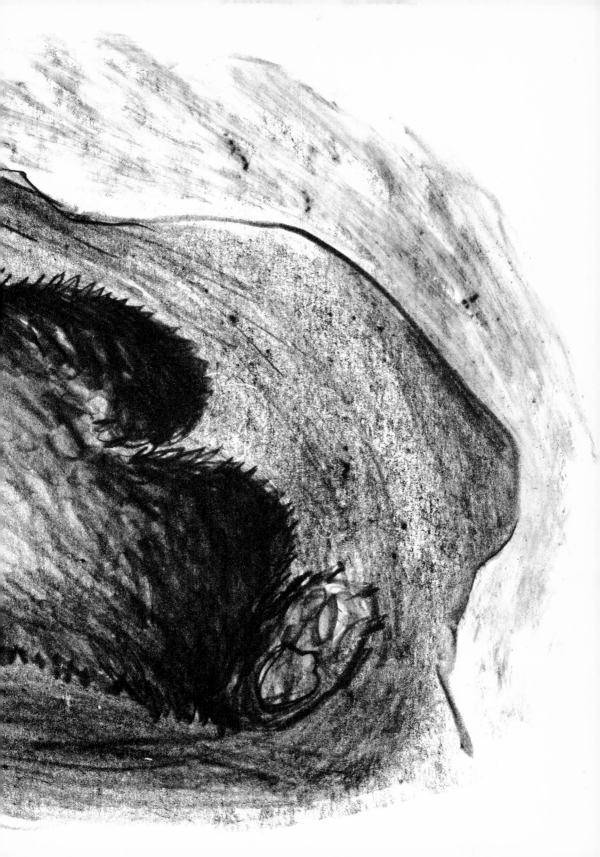

he fell on his back. But the little water-sprite managed to get away to his father and tell him what had happened. "He must be strong, that boy. His old grandfather is so strong that when he struck me on the shoulder I almost fell to pieces."

"Ah, if he is such a dangerous chap," said the water-sprite, "you had better go up and ask him how much money he wants to leave us alone."

The wee water-sprite went up again, as his father ordered, and asked the boy how much money he would demand to leave the lake alone.

"Enough to fill my hat," the boy answered, and put his hat on the ground.

The little water-sprite ran back to the lake and fetched a great weight of money. Meanwhile the boy had cut a hole in the crown of his hat and dug a pit under it. When the wee water-sprite poured the coins into the hat, they of course ran down into the pit. He had to go back to his father to fetch some more.

"There was only enough to cover the bottom of the hat," said the little water-sprite.

"Take a barrelful this time," answered the water-sprite. "You can tell him that it is almost all the money I have."

The wee water-sprite dragged the barrelful of coins up through the lake and offered it to the boy. "It is almost all the money we have," he said.

The boy now was satisfied. He promised not to tie up the lake. When he went home to the old cottage and his brothers saw what he had brought with him, they couldn't believe their eyes.

"How on earth did you find so much money?" they asked.

"By catching animals," he answered. "When you left me with nothing but the pile of rope, I made snares and began to catch animals. That is how I have become so rich."

"Take the cottage, then, and all that is in it, and give us the rope," cried the two brothers.

The boy did as they demanded. The brothers made snares from the rope and went off to catch animals. To this day they must still be doing this. But whether they have become richer or not, no one knows.

The Old Woman and the Tramp

A TRAMP WAS ONCE plodding along on his way through a forest. The distance between the houses there was so great that he knew he had little hope of finding shelter before night set in. But all of a sudden he saw bright lights shining between the trees. He discovered a cottage with a brisk fire burning on the hearth. How good it would be, he thought, to toast himself before that blaze, and to find a bite of food! With this in mind, he dragged himself over to the cottage.

An old woman appeared at the door.

"Good evening, and well met!" said the tramp.

"Good evening," said the woman. "And where do you come from?"

"South of the sun, and east of the moon," said

the tramp. "And now I am on the way home again, for I have been all over the world except in this parish."

"You must be a great traveler indeed," said the woman. "What may be your business here?"

"Oh, I want only a shelter for the night."

"I thought as much," said the woman. "But you may as well go away at once, for my husband is not at home and my cottage is not an inn."

"My good woman," said the tramp, "you must not be so hard-hearted. We are both human beings. It is written that we should help one another."

"Help one another?" said the woman. "Help? Did you ever hear of such a thing? Who will help me, do you think? I haven't a morsel in the house! No, you must look for shelter elsewhere."

But the tramp was like the rest of his kind. He would not consider himself beaten at the first rebuff. Although the old woman grumbled, he kept at it. He begged like a starved dog, until at

last she gave in and granted him permission to lie on the floor for the night.

That was very kind, he thought, and he thanked her for it.

"It is better to lie on the floor without sleep than to suffer cold in the forest deep," he said. He was a merry fellow, this tramp, and always ready with a rhyming word.

When he entered the cottage he could see that the woman was not so badly off as she had pretended to be. She was just stingy and complaining.

The tramp tried to make himself agreeable as he asked her for something to eat.

"Where shall I get it?" asked the woman. "I haven't tasted a morsel the whole day."

But the tramp was a cunning fellow, he was.

"Poor old granny, you must be starving. Well, well, I suppose I shall have to ask you to have something with me, then."

"Have something with you!" said the woman.

"You don't look as if you could ask anyone to have anything! What have you to offer, I should like to know?"

"He who far and wide does roam sees many things not known at home; and he who many things has seen has wits about him and senses keen," said the tramp, with more of his rhymes. "Better dead than to lose one's head! Lend me a pot, granny!"

The old woman had now grown curious, as you may guess. She let him have a big pot.

The tramp filled the pot with water and hung it over the fire. Then he blew and blew till the fire flared up brightly all around it. He took a four-inch nail from his pocket, carefully turned it around three times in his hand, and dropped it into the pot.

The woman stared. "What is this going to be?" she asked.

"Nail broth," said the tramp, and began to stir the water with the porridge whisk.

"Nail broth?" asked the woman.

"Yes, nail broth," said the tramp.

The old woman had seen and heard a good deal in her time, but that anybody could make broth with a nail, well, she had never heard the like of this before.

"That's something for poor people to know," she said, "and I should like to learn how to make it."

"That which is not worth having will always go a-begging," said the tramp.

But if she wanted to learn to make it she had only to watch him, he said, and went on stirring the broth.

The old woman squatted near the hearth, her hands clasping her knees and her eyes following the tramp's hand as he stirred the broth.

"This generally makes good broth," he said; "but this time it will very likely be rather thin, for this whole week I have been making broth with the same nail. If only I had a handful of sifted meal to add, that would make it all right. But what one has to go without, it's no use thinking more about," and once again he stirred the broth.

"Well, I think I have a scrap of flour somewhere," said the old woman. She went to fetch it, and it was both good and fine.

The tramp began stirring the flour into the broth and went on stirring and stirring, while the woman sat, staring now at him and then at the pot, until her eyes seemed nearly to burst from their sockets.

"This broth would be good enough for company," the tramp now announced, putting in one handful of flour after another, "if only I had a bit of salted beef and a few potatoes to add. Indeed, it would be fit for gentlefolk, however particular they might be. But what one has to go without, it's no use thinking more about."

The old woman began to consider this, and she remembered she had a few potatoes, and perhaps there was a bit of beef as well. These she found and gave to the tramp, who went on stirring and stirring, while she sat and stared as hard as ever.

"This will be grand enough for the best in the land," he said at last.

"Well, I never!" said the woman. "And just fancy — all that with a nail!"

"If we had only a little barley and a drop of milk, we could ask the King himself to sup some of this. This is what he has every evening. That I know, for I have been in service under the King's cook," he said.

"Dear me! Ask the King to have some! Well, I never!" exclaimed the woman, slapping her knees. She was quite overcome by the tramp and his grand connections.

"But what one has to go without, it's no use thinking more about," said the tramp.

And then the woman remembered she had a a little barley. And as for milk, well, she wasn't quite out of that, she said, for her best cow had just calved. She went to fetch both the one and the other.

The tramp went on with his stirring, and the woman with her staring, one moment at him and the next at the pot.

Suddenly the tramp took out the nail.

"Now it's ready, and we'll have a real feast. But with this kind of soup the King and the Queen always have something to drink, and one sandwich at least. And then they always have a cloth on the table when they eat," he added. "But what one has to go without, it's no use thinking more about."

By this time the old woman herself had begun to feel quite grand, I can tell you. If that was all that was wanted to make the soup just as the King had it, she thought it would be nice to have it just the same way for once, and play at being King and Queen with the tramp. So she went to a cupboard and brought out a bottle and glasses, butter and cheese, smoked beef and veal, until at last the table looked as if it were decked out for company.

Never in her life had the old woman eaten such a grand feast, and never had she tasted such broth. Just fancy, made only with a nail! She was in such a merry humor at having learned such an economical way of making broth that she could not do enough for the tramp who had taught her such a useful thing.

The old woman and the tramp then ate and drank, and drank and ate, until their hunger was satisfied.

The tramp was ready to lie down on the floor to sleep. But that would never do, thought the old woman. No, that was impossible. Such a grand person must have a bed to lie in.

The tramp did not need much urging. "It's just like the sweet Christmas time. Happy are they who meet such good people." And he lay on the bed she offered him and went to sleep.

Next morning when the tramp awoke, the old woman was ready with coffee for him. And as he was leaving, she gave him a bright dollar piece.

"And thanks, many thanks, for what you have taught me," she said. "Now I shall live in comfort, since I have learned how to make broth with a nail."

"Well, it isn't very difficult, if one only has something good to add to it," said the tramp as he went on his way.

The woman stood at the door staring after him.

"Such people don't grow on every bush," she said.

The Lad and the Fox

ONCE UPON A TIME there was a little lad who was on his way to church through a forest. When he came to a clearing, he caught sight of a fox. The fox was lying on the top of a big stone so fast asleep that he did not know the lad had seen him.

"If I kill that fox," said the lad, taking a heavy stone in his fist, "and sell the skin, I shall get money for it. And with that money I shall buy some rye seed, and that rye I shall sow in Father's field at home. When the people on their way to church pass by my field of rye they will say, 'What splendid rye that lad has grown!' Then I shall say to them, 'I say, keep away from my rye!'

"But they won't heed me, so I shall *shout* to them, 'I say, keep away from my rye!' But still they won't take any notice of me. Then I shall *scream* with all my might, 'Keep away from my rye!' and they will listen to me."

The lad screamed so loudly now that the fox woke up. He made off at once for the forest, so the lad did not get as much as a handful of the fox's hair.

No, it is best always to take what you can reach. Of undone deeds you should never screech.

Pinkel

ONCE UPON A TIME there lived a poor widow with her three sons. The two eldest sons went out to work and were seldom at home with their old mother. Perhaps this was just as well, because they never did what she asked them to do. But the youngest son stayed at home and helped his mother with all the work. He was therefore much beloved by her. This made his brothers hate him and give him the nickname of Pinkel.

One day the poor widow said to her sons, "The time has come when you must all three go out into the world to seek your fortunes. You are too old to live at home any longer."

The three lads were pleased with this idea, and after packing their few possessions they set off.

When they had traveled a long time without finding any work, they came one evening to a big lake. Far out on the lake they saw an island on which blazed a light like a huge fire. The brothers stopped to look at the strange light and agreed that there must be people on the island. As it was already dark and they had found no shelter, they stepped into a boat that lay in the reeds and rowed over to the island, to see if they could find a roof for the night.

When they arrived, they found a little cottage near the shore. They discovered that the beautiful light they had seen came from a golden lantern hung in the doorway of the cottage. In the yard wandered a large goat with golden horns, and on its horns were fastened many small bells which tinkled when it moved. This surprised

the brothers, but even more surprising was the old hag who lived there with her daughter. She was foul and ugly, yet she wore a costly coat so cleverly knit with golden threads that it shone like purest gold. The three brothers knew that she must be a witch and not an ordinary person.

In spite of these strange sights, the three

brothers decided to enter the cottage. They found the witch standing by the fire, stirring her porridge, and they asked if they might spend the night.

The witch would not take them in, but told them to go to the King's castle, which lay on the other side of the lake. As she was telling them this, she looked sharply at Pinkel, who was gazing around the cottage.

"What are you called, boy?" she asked.

"Pinkel," was his answer.

"Your brothers may go their way, but I want you to stay here. You look far brighter than they and I know that you will do me no good if I let you go to the King's palace."

Pinkel begged to follow his brothers and promised never to do the old witch any harm. At length she allowed him to join his brothers, and all three rowed away from the island, happy to have escaped.

Next morning the brothers came to the King's

palace, which was more grand and beautiful than any they had ever imagined. They entered and asked if there were work that they could do. The two eldest thereupon were made stableboys and Pinkel became the King's page boy. Pinkel proved so brisk and bright at his work that he soon rose high in the King's favor. This vexed his two brothers and they began to plot how to get rid of him.

One day the two went to the King and told him about the beautiful lantern. The King listened and asked, "Where is this lantern and who can get it for me?"

"Our youngest brother, Pinkel, knows best where to find it," they answered.

The King so craved to own the lantern that he sent Pinkel to get it, telling him that if he could bring it to the castle he, the King, would promote Pinkel to the most important position at court.

When Pinkel reached the island it was evening

and the witch stood as before in front of her fire stirring her porridge. Quietly Pinkel climbed onto the cottage roof and threw a handful of salt down the chimney into the pot. This made the porridge so salty that the witch was unable to eat it. Grumbling, she sent her daughter to fetch water from the well so that she could cook some more porridge. The girl went out into the dark, taking with her the golden lantern. As she leaned over the well, Pinkel pushed her into the water, and with the golden lantern in his boat rowed quickly away from the island.

The witch, wondering why her daughter was so slow, looked out and saw the light shining far off on the lake. Alarmed, she ran out and shrieked, "Is that you, Pinkel?"

"Why, yes, it is, old mother!" answered Pinkel.

"Have you taken my lantern?" she asked.

"Why, yes, I have taken it, old mother!" answered Pinkel.

"You are a rogue, aren't you?" shouted the witch.

"Why, yes, I am, old mother!" replied Pinkel.

"I knew you would trick me," screamed the hag, "but next time you won't win!"

So Pinkel returned to the King's palace and became first man at court, which made his brothers even more spiteful than before. Again they went to the King and this time told him about the goat with the golden horns and tinkling bells. At once, the King sent for Pinkel and offered him one third of his kingdom if he could bring back this wonderful goat.

The island was completely dark when Pinkel reached it this time, because there was no lantern with golden light. Pinkel pondered how he could reach the goat, for it slept inside the cottage, and at bedtime the witch always locked her door. Pinkel, however, stuck a splint of wood in the doorway, which made it impossible for them to lock the door.

In the middle of the night, when everyone lay sleeping, Pinkel crept in, stuffed the goat's bells with wool and carried the animal to the boat. When he had rowed far out on the lake, he removed the wool mufflers and allowed the bells to chime. The witch awoke, ran down to the shore and, as before, called out to Pinkel that next time she would catch him for sure.

So Pinkel returned to the King's palace and received his award of one third of the King's domain. Now his brothers were raging with envy. They went again to the King and told him about the witch's shining coat which was knit of golden thread. The King knew he had to have this coat, so he said to Pinkel, "I have known for a long time that you love my daughter. If you will bring me the shining gold coat, you may have her to wed and inherit all of my kingdom as well."

As Pinkel rowed away for the third time on a mission for the King, he wondered how he should manage to get the golden coat. It would not be

easy, for the witch always wore her coat. Finally, however, he hit upon a plan.

Pinkel tied a bag under his coat and walked into the cottage pretending to be humble and afraid. The witch looked at him with a piercing eye.

"Is that you, Pinkel?"

"Why, yes, it is, little mother!" he answered.

"Now that you are at my mercy, I shall kill you," the old witch said, and she picked up a knife.

When Pinkel saw this, he begged, "Since I am to die, please let me choose how. Let me eat myself to death."

The old witch thought that he had chosen a painful way to die, so she agreed. She went to the fire and cooked a pot full of porridge. When it was ready Pinkel began to eat. But for each mouthful he swallowed, he put two in the bag concealed beneath his coat. After a while, he pretended to be ill and rolled on the floor. The witch

ran out, calling for her daughter, the one who before had been pushed into the well. Because rain was pouring down, the witch had taken off her coat. The moment she was out of the door, Pinkel picked up the coat and ran to his boat.

When the witch saw that Pinkel had tricked her a third time, she called out furiously.

"You are a villain, aren't you, Pinkel?"

"Why, yes, so I am, old mother!" shouted Pinkel.

Pinkel, bearing the shining coat, returned joyfully to the King's castle. He was proclaimed a Prince and married the lovely Princess. And when the old King died, Pinkel inherited the kingdom — but his two brothers remained stableboys all of their lives.

The Old Woman and the Fish

ONCE UPON A TIME an old woman lived in a poor cottage on the brow of a hill overlooking a town. Her husband had been dead for many years and her children were in service round about the parish, so she felt rather lonely and dreary in her cottage.

All the old woman could console herself with was that one must be satisfied. But the pails of water which she had to carry up the hill from the well were so heavy. And her ax had such a blunt and rusty edge. It was only with the greatest difficulty that she could cut a little firewood. And the cloth she was weaving was not long enough. All this grieved her, and caused her to complain from time to time.

One day when she had pulled her bucket up from the well she found a small pike in it, which did not displease her a bit.

"Such a fish does not come into my pot every day," she said. Now she would have a really grand dish to eat, she thought. But the fish which she had got this time was no fool. It had the gift of speech, that it had.

"Let me go!" said the fish.

The old woman began to stare. Such a fish she had never before seen.

"Are you so much better than other fish, then?" she said, "and too good to be eaten?"

"Wise is he who does not eat all he gets hold of," said the fish; "only let me go and you shall not remain without reward for your trouble."

"I like a fish in the bucket better than all those frisking about free and frolicsome in the lakes," said the old woman. "And what one can catch with one hand one can also carry to one's mouth."

"That may be," said the fish; "but if you do as I tell you, you shall have three wishes."

"Promises are well enough," said the woman, "but keeping them is better, and I shall not believe in you till I have got you in the pot."

"You should mind that tongue of yours," said the fish, "and listen to my words. Wish for three things, and then you'll see what will happen."

Well, the old woman knew well enough what she wanted to wish. There might not be so much danger in trying to see how far the fish would keep his word.

She began thinking of the long climb up the hill from the well.

"I would wish that my pails could go of themselves to the well and home again," she said.

"So they shall," said the fish.

Then she thought of her ax, and how blunt it was.

"I would wish that whatever I strike shall break right off," she said.

"So it shall," said the fish.

And then she remembered that the stuff she was weaving was not long enough.

"I would wish that whatever I pull shall become long," she said.

"That it shall," said the fish. "And now, let me down into the well again."

Yes, that she would. And all at once the pails began to shamble up the hill.

"Dear me, did you ever see anything like it?" The old woman became so pleased that she slapped herself across the knees.

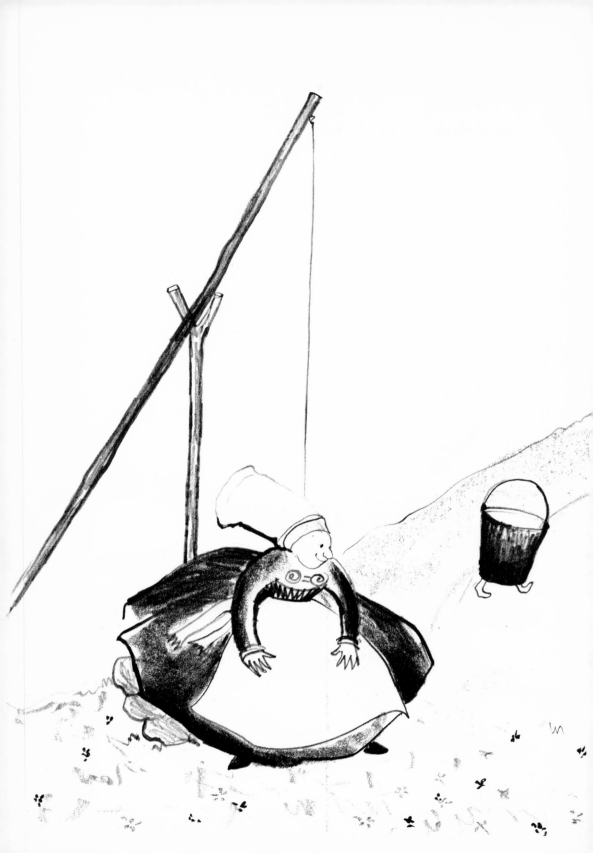

Crack, crack this sounded; and both of her legs fell off. She was left sitting on top of the lid over the well.

Now she began to cry, and the tears ran down her face. She began blowing her nose in her apron, and as she tugged at her nose it grew so long that it was strange to behold.

That is what she got for her wishes! There she sat, and there she no doubt still sits on the lid of the well. And if you want to know what it is to have a long nose, you had better go there and ask her, for she can tell you all about it, she can.

Lars, My Lad!

THERE WAS ONCE a Prince who left home to travel all over the world. And wherever he went he was well liked and was received by the finest families, for he had no end of money.

Wherever he went he made friends and spent his money gaily, until he had not even one farthing left. And now there was an end to all his friendships. Everybody had been willing to help him spend his money, but nobody would help him in return. There was nothing for it but he must trudge home, begging for crusts on the way.

Late one evening he came to a great forest. He kept on walking till he spied a tumbledown hut in the middle of a patch of bushes. It was not a suitable shelter for such a fine young man, but since there was no help for it, the Prince entered the hut. No one was to be seen. There was no stool to sit upon, but alongside one wall stood a big chest. What could there be in it? The Prince hoped he might find food there, for he had not eaten all day and was so hungry that his stomach groaned with pain. He lifted the lid.

Inside the chest was another chest, and in that another. And so it continued to be; in each chest was one smaller, until they became tiny boxes. The more he opened, the harder he worked at it. He felt there must be something valuable inside, to be so well hidden.

At last the Prince came to a miniature box in which lay a tiny piece of paper. That was all he found, for all his trouble! It disappointed him, but then he discovered something written on the paper. He was just able to make out the words *Lars, my lad!*

As he pronounced these words, he heard

someone answer — right in his ear — "What are Master's orders?"

The Prince looked around, but he saw nobody. This was strange. He read out the words once more, "Lars, my lad!"

And the answer came as before, "What are Master's orders?"

He did not see anyone this time, either.

"If there is anybody about who hears what I say, then be kind enough to bring me something to eat," he asked.

The very next moment, there stood a table laid out with all the best things one could think of. The Prince ate and drank and thought he had never enjoyed himself so much in all his life.

When he had eaten all he could, he began to feel sleepy. He took out the paper again and said, "Lars, my lad!"

"What are Master's orders?" was the answer again.

"You have given me food and drink aplenty; now you must find me a bed to sleep in. But I want a really fine bed," he added. He was a bit more bold now that his hunger was satisfied.

Well, there it stood, a bed so fine that even the King himself might covet it.

This was all very well in its way, but when you become well off you wish for still more. No sooner had the Prince climbed into bed than he began to think that the room itself was altogether too poor for such a grand bed. Out came the paper again, and the words, "Lars, my lad!"

"What are Master's orders?" was the answer once more.

"Since you are able to supply me with such food and such a fine bed here in this forest, I am sure you can get me a better room. You see, I am accustomed to sleeping in a palace, with golden mirrors and covered walls, and ornaments and comforts of all kinds."

Well, no sooner had he spoken these words

than he found himself lying in the most lavish chamber that anybody has ever seen.

Now, thought the Prince, he could be comfortable. He turned his face to the wall and closed his eyes to sleep, feeling quite satisfied.

But he had not yet seen all the grandeur. When he awoke and looked around in the morning, he saw that he had been sleeping in a great palace. He found that one room led into another, and wherever he turned he saw rich furnishings. The walls and ceilings glittered so with gold and silver that he had to shade his eyes when the sun shone on them.

Next he looked out of the windows. What grandeur out of doors, too! — not pine forests and juniper bushes any longer, but a garden with rare trees and roses of every kind.

Still the Prince could not see one human being, nor even a cat, and that made him lonely.

He took out the bit of paper and said again, "Lars, my lad!"

"What are Master's orders?" he heard again.

"Well, now that you have given me food and a bed, and a fine palace to live in, I intend to remain here, for I like the place. But I don't wish to live alone here. I must have both lads and lasses whom I may order about, to wait on me."

At once, there they were! — stewards and serving women, scullery maids and chambermaids. Some came bowing, some curtseying. Now the Prince thought he was satisfied.

But it happened that there was a large palace on the other side of the forest. As the King who owned it happened to look out of his window on waking, he saw the new palace. Golden weathercocks swung to and fro on its roof, dazzling his eyes.

"This is strange," he thought. He called his courtiers, who rushed in, bowing and scraping before him.

"Who is it that has dared to build such a palace on my land?" asked the King.

The courtiers bowed, and they scraped with their feet, but they did not know the answer.

The King then called his generals and captains. These came, stood at attention, and presented arms.

"Begone, soldiers," said the King, "and pull down that palace. Hang him who has built it, and don't lose any time about it!"

Well, they set off in haste to arm themselves, and away they went. The drummers beat the skins of their drums, and the trumpeters blew their trumpets, and the other musicians played and blew as best they could, so that the Prince heard them long before he could see them. But he had heard that kind of noise before, and knew what it meant. He took out his scrap of paper and said, "Lars, my lad!"

"What are Master's orders?" he heard.

"There are soldiers coming here. You must provide me with soldiers and horses, that I may have double as many as those over in the wood.

They must have sabers and pistols, and guns and cannon; but be quick about it."

No time was lost. When the Prince looked out, he beheld an immense number of soldiers drawn up around the palace.

When the King's men arrived, they came to a sudden halt and dared not advance nearer. The Prince was not afraid. He went straight to the officer in charge of the King's soldiers and asked him what he wanted.

The officer told him.

"It's of no use," said the Prince. "You can see how many men I have. If the King will listen to me, we can become good friends. I will be glad to help him against his enemies, and in such a way that this will be heard of far and wide."

The officer agreed with the Prince, and the Prince invited him and his men inside the palace, where he feasted them well.

While they were dining, they began to talk. The Prince thus learned that the King had a

daughter, who was his only child. She was so wonderfully fair that no one had seen her like before. The more the soldiers ate and drank, the more they thought she would suit the Prince well for a wife.

They talked so long that the Prince began to be of the same opinion as the King's men. "But," said the soldiers, "she is as proud as she is beautiful. She will never look at a man."

The Prince only laughed at this. "If that is all, there is sure to be a remedy."

When the soldiers could eat no more, they set out homewards. Before they left the Prince made sure to ask them to greet the King for him and say that he would call on him the next day.

When the Prince was alone again, he began to think of the Princess and to wonder if she could be as beautiful as the soldiers had said. He must make sure of it. So many strange things had happened that day; it might be possible to find that out, he thought.

"Lars, my lad!"

"What are Master's orders?"

"You must bring me the King's daughter as soon as she has gone to sleep, but she must not be awakened either on the way here or on the way back. Do you hear that?" he asked.

Before long the Princess was lying on a bed before him. She was sleeping soundly and looked exquisitely beautiful as she lay there.

The Prince walked all around her. He found her to be just as lovely from one side as from another.

The more he looked at her, the more he liked her.

"Lars, my lad!"

"What are Master's orders?"

"You must now carry the Princess home," he said, "for now I know how she looks, and tomorrow I will ask for her hand."

Next morning the King looked out of the window. "I suppose I shall not be troubled with the sight of that palace any more," he thought. But, zounds! There it stood just as on the day before. With the sun shining brightly on its roof, the golden weathercocks dazzled his eyes again.

He became furious, and called his men.

More quickly than usual, in they came.

The courtiers bowed and scraped, and the soldiers stood at attention and presented arms.

"Do you see that palace?" screamed the King.

The courtiers and soldiers stared and gaped. Yes, of course, they saw it.

"Did I not order you to pull down the palace and hang the builder?" he cried.

They could not deny this, but they reported what had happened and how many soldiers the Prince had. Also they reported how the Prince had asked them to give his greetings to the King.

The King was confused. He had to put his crown on the table and scratch his head. Although he was a King, he could not understand this. He knew that the palace had been built in but a single night. It must have been magic that created it.

While the King was pondering this, the Princess came into the room.

"Good morning, Father. Just fancy, I had such a strange and beautiful dream last night!"

"What did you dream, my girl?" asked the King.

"I dreamed that I was in that new palace over yonder, and that I saw a Prince there so handsome that I could never have imagined his like. Now I want to get married, Father."

"You want to get married! You, who have never cared to look at a man! That's very strange!" said the King.

"That may be," said the Princess. "But it's different now. I want to get married, and it's that Prince I want."

The King was quite beside himself, so frightened was he of the Prince and his magic.

All of a sudden he heard a great sound of

drums and trumpets. Then came a message that the Prince had arrived with a large company of followers, all so grandly dressed that gold and silver glistened in every fold of their garments. The King put on his crown and his fine coronation robes and went out on the palace steps to receive the Prince and his retinue. The Princess was not slow to follow her father.

The Prince bowed most graciously, and the King of course did the same. When they had discussed their affairs and their grandeur, they appeared to have become the best of friends. A great banquet was prepared and the Prince was seated next to the Princess. The Prince spoke so well for himself that the Princess could not say no to anything he said.

The Prince then went to the King and asked for the hand of the Princess. The King could not very well say no either, but before settling matters, he wanted to see the Prince's palace. So it was arranged that the King should visit the

Prince and take the Princess with him to see the new palace.

When the Prince returned home, Lars became busier than ever, for there was much to attend to. When the King and his daughter arrived they found everything so magnificent that words could not describe it. The King appeared pleased.

The wedding was celebrated in grand style, and when the Prince arrived home with his bride, he, too, gave a great feast.

Time passed. One evening the Prince heard the words, "Are you satisfied now?"

It was Lars, as you may guess, but the Prince could not see him.

"Well, I ought to be," said the Prince. "You have provided me with everything."

"Yes, but what have I received in return?" asked Lars.

"Nothing," said the Prince, "but, bless me, what could I have given you, who are not of flesh and blood, and whom I cannot see? If there

is anything I can do for you, tell me what it is, and I shall do it."

"Well, I should like that little scrap of paper which you found in the chest," said Lars.

"Nothing else?" said the Prince. "If such a trifle can help you, I can easily do without it, for now I know the words by heart."

Lars thanked the Prince, and asked him to put the paper on the chair in front of his bed when he retired. He would get it during the night.

The Prince did as he was told, then he and the Princess went to sleep.

Early in the morning the Prince awoke, so cold that his teeth chattered. When he opened his eyes, he found he had not a stitch on his back. Instead of lying on a grand bed in a beautiful bedroom within a magnificent palace, he lay on the big chest in the old hut.

The Prince began to shout, "Lars, my lad!" but he got no answer. He shouted once more,

"Lars, my lad!" but got no answer this time either. So he shouted as loud as he could, "*Lars, my lad!*" It was all in vain.

Now the Prince began to understand. When Lars had the scrap of paper, he became freed from service, and he had taken everything with him.

There was no help for it. The Princess had only her clothes. She had got them from her father, and Lars had no power over them.

The Prince had to tell the Princess how everything had happened, and he asked her to leave him. He would have to manage as best he could, he said. But the Princess would not hear of it. She remembered well what the parson had said when he married them. She would never, never leave her husband.

In the meantime, the King in his palace had also awakened, and when he looked out of his window he did not see the Prince's palace. He became uneasy, and he called his courtiers.

The courtiers trooped in, and began to bow and scrape.

"Do you see the palace over yonder behind the forest?" asked the King.

The men stared with all their might.

No, they did not see it.

"Where has it gone to, then?" asked the King.

Well, really they did not know.

It was not long before the King was on his way with his court. When they arrived where the palace should have been, they could see nothing but heather and juniper bushes. But among the bushes the King discovered the old hut. He entered and found his son-in-law, and his daughter weeping and moaning.

"Dear, dear! What does all this mean?" asked the King. But he did not get an answer, for the Prince could not bring himself to tell the King what had happened.

In spite of the King's promises and threats, the Prince remained silent.

The King became angry, for he could see that this Prince was not what he pretended to be. He ordered the Prince to be hanged, and at once. The Princess begged that mercy be shown the Prince, but neither her prayers nor her tears were of any help. An impostor should be hanged, said the King.

So it was to be.

The Prince had time to reflect on how foolish he had been in not saving some of the crumbs when he was living in plenty. And how stupid he had been in letting Lars have the scrap of paper. If only he had it again! They should see that he had gained some sense in return for all he had lost.

Just before the sun set in the forest, the Prince heard a great shouting. When he looked, he saw seven cartloads of worn-out shoes, and on top of the hindmost cart he spied a little old man in gray with a red pointed cap on his head. His face was like that of a poor scarecrow, and the rest of him not handsome either.

Straight he drove to the gallows where the Prince was awaiting his end. He looked at the Prince, and burst out laughing.

"How stupid you were! What should a fool do with his stupidity if he did not make use of it?" Then he laughed again. "Yes, there you are, and here am I carting away all the shoes I have worn out for your whims. I wonder if you can read what is written on this bit of paper, and if you recognize it?" With an ugly laugh, he held up the paper before the Prince's eyes.

This time it was Lars who was the fool, for the Prince, although he had a rope about his neck, snatched the paper from him.

"Lars, my lad!"

"What are Master's orders?"

"You must cut this rope and put the palace and all the rest in place again, exactly as before.

And when night has come, you must bring back the Princess."

All went merrily as in a dance, and before long everything was in its place.

When the King awoke the next morning, he looked out of the window as usual. There stood the palace again with its weathercocks glittering beautifully in the sunshine. He called his courtiers at once.

"Do you see the palace over there?" asked the King.

Yes, of course they did.

The King sent for the Princess, but she was not to be found. He went out to see if his son-in-law was hanging, but neither son-in-law nor gallows were to be seen.

At once the King set off through the forest. When he came to the place where the palace should stand, there it stood, sure enough. The gardens and the roses were exactly as they used to be, and the Prince's attendants. The Prince

and the Princess, dressed in their finest, received
the King.

"Well, I never saw the like of this," said the
King to himself. He could not believe his eyes.

"God's peace be with you, Father, and wel-
come here!" said the Prince.

The King stared at him.

"Are you my son-in-law?" he asked.

"Well, I suppose I am," said the Prince. "Who
else could I be?"

"Did I not order you to be hanged yesterday
like any common thief?" asked the King.

"I think you must have been bewitched on
the way," said the Prince with a laugh. "Do you
think I am the man to allow myself to be hanged?
Or does anyone here dare to believe it? If anyone dares to say the King could have wished me
such evil, let him speak," said the Prince.

How could anyone dare to say such a thing?
No, they hoped they had more sense than that.

The King did not know what to believe, for

when he looked at the Prince he thought he could never have wished him evil. But still he was not quite convinced.

"Did I not come here yesterday, and was not the whole palace gone, and was there not an old hut standing in its place? And did I not go into that hut and see you there?"

"I wonder that the King can talk so," said the Prince. "I think the trolls must have bewitched your eyes and made you crazy. Or what do *you* think?" he said, and turned around to the King's courtiers.

These all bowed till their backs were bent double, and agreed with everything he said. The King rubbed his eyes, and looked round him.

"I suppose it is as you say, then," he said to the Prince. "It is well I have got back my proper sight and have come to my senses again, for it would have been a shame to have let you be hanged." He was happy again, and nobody thought any more about the matter.

The Prince now took it upon himself to manage his affairs, so that it was seldom Lars had to wear down his shoes. The King soon gave the Prince half of his kingdom, so he had plenty to do. People began to say that they would have to search a long time to find his equal in wisdom and justice.

One day Lars came to the Prince, looking very little better than before. But this time he was more humble, and did not dare to giggle and make faces.

"You do not want my help any longer," he said. "But I used to wear out my shoes, now I am unable to do so. My feet will soon be covered with moss. Now perhaps you might let me go."

The Prince agreed. "I have tried to spare you, and I almost think I could do without you. But the palace and all the rest I do not want to lose, for such a clever builder as you I shall never get again. I cannot give you back the paper on any account."

"Well," said Lars, "as long as you have it, I need not fear; but if anybody else should get it, there would be nothing but running about again, and that's what I want to avoid. When one has been tramping about as I have done, one begins to tire of it."

At last they agreed that the Prince should put the paper in the box and bury it twenty feet under the ground, beneath a stone. They then thanked one another and parted.

The Prince carried out his part of the agreement, which he was not likely to want to change. He and the Princess lived happily and had both sons and daughters. When the King died, the Prince inherited the whole of the kingdom, and he reigns there still, if he is not dead.

As for that box with the scrap of paper in it, there are many who are still running about looking for it.

19545
49

J
398   H
HAVILAND
   FAVORITE FAIRY TALES TOLD
IN SWEDEN   2.97

DISCARD

4